I0445780

SKAGEN

SKAGEN

a short novel by

JEAN COQT

translated from the french by

charles lunaire

the first part of

Skagen a novel of Europe

Translator's dedication

This book is truly for the woman who has been at my side for nearly sixty years, across Europe from north to south, from west to east, on foot, on bicycle, in trains and buses, in autos, bed and breakfast, rain and shine. The companion of my life, and whatever meaning there may be. Everything. *Rien sans toi.*

Copyright ©2013 EarPress

first edition

all rights reserved

ISBN: 978 0 9907588 0 8

Healdsburg : Ear Press : 2014

C o n t e n t s

1. Flies covering the dinnertable

There where ripples from one direction crossed through those from the
*   other*
each proceeding in a measured pace driven by who knows what events
breezes today storms perhaps tomorrow
walking out on the strand (joycean word) with nothing in mind but
sand underfoot (what walking shoes those days?) sea on both sides
nostalgic paintings in the museum: women and girls
fine summer dresses, long skirts
parasols held gracefully aloft blue sky
warm sunlight filtering through onto fair skin
eyes blue to be sure slim figures
healthy long legs none over thirty
summer days, unseen workers, empty streets
cool spacious museum quiet lady at desk
helpful but taciturn, not much english
brisk crossing to sweden

HE CARRIES THESE memories, no, thoughts, from the farm to the ferry dock:

Flies covering the dinnertable in the farmhouse, and the unconcern with which the family eats supper. Somewhat strained conversation, the older generation effectively monolingual each in his own language, only the youngsters able to any degree to deal with both, and they not particularly interested. The little house in Harritslev where he wrote such a fond adieu. Somehow the narrow country roads lazing through green hills of pasture. The trip to the dunes, dunes like all those running south through Friesland, Holland, West Flanderen, Normandy. Lighthouses, or is he thinking of Ré. Horse-breeding.

Girls and women looking on, waiting, poised, attentive: the men either absent or intent. In general, of course. All hopelessly generalized, don't you agree?   Only a novelist would pretend insight, let alone omniscience. Point of view.

Everything unfamiliar and new no matter how often sampled before. And the contrast of public and personal. The first trip relying entirely on public transportation. In a car even if not alone you are centered within yourself: on a tram or walking in the city you constantly — you're aware whether consciously or not of a distinction between yourself and everyone else around you. Not the distinction you find sitting in an audience at the theater or the concert hall, or at a baseball game, or pushing your cart through the supermarket: there you're part of a collective. On the tram it's you alone and all the others. You might catch one of them if you're quick. Now and then one will make some little gesture, some little sound, drawing your attention — who is it catching whom?   — and he's detached too from his collective otherness-from-you.   This is likely to embarrass him. He'll look down at his shoes for no reason, or adjust her purse, or rummage about in a pocket. Handkerchief, notebook, eyeglasses.   Pocket mirror: checking her own nose, or glancing behind her?

Plane touched down on time, seven forty: uneventful trip somehow into city center: some hotel or another. Familiar with Amsterdam and The Hague, Copenhagen is similar:

but everything unfamiliar and new no matter how often sampled before, and the language… They found a hotel, probably asking at a tourist desk somewhere — airport, where they cashed a travelers check for bus money? Or in the city, where they cashed another, thinking they'd get a better exchange rate? Lunch at a bistro. Is it worth looking at old photos? Later. What he likes: walkabout. Shop windows, *trottoirs*, trams, small collections of unfamiliar people, their clothing and manner recalling San Francisco of the late 1940s. A quieter time.

Dinner at the Lido, then a stroll through the Tivoli Gardens — what else would you do in Copenhagen? The sun will set late, we're nearing Midsummer. The park is oddly full, well, not full, but beset by drunk children. Ten or twelve years old, not yet adolescent, running about uncontrolled and uncontrollable, quite drunk, shouting and running. No idea what they're shouting: drunk or sober, Danish is incomprehensible. Ah: it's Friday: today was the last day of school.   On the bus ride into the city we'd noticed schoolbags hanging from flagpoles.   That's what it's all about. Disturbing.

2. The two sides of the road

BUT THAT WAS days ago. Since then, train: Århus, Hjørring, Harritslev, Skagen. And the farm across the road, only its dairy-barn and farmhouse kitchen visited, the M family mysterious and unknown. Far, the father: lean, suspicious, insecure. Mor, the mother: also small, pretty-but-plain, reserved. Søster: quiet and suspicious. Absent son. Big black dog, woolly, floppy, friendly, goofy.

The little cottage, stone and wood, low for hunkering down in the Jutland winters no doubt, with a pleasant day-room, a small kitchen, a comfortable bedroom and adequate bath.

You get about by bicycle. The days are warm and sunny, the landscape gentle, rolling, bovine. Still you carry those farmers with you. They want to be available, socially as well as physically, but don't know how. Only much later, on reflection, can you imagine how odd and unapproachable you are, big, rangy, taking up too much space, loud at rare but unpredictable moments. *Effort. Effortful. Effortfulness.*

The two sides of the road: dairy: cottage. Sunlight streaming into bedroom in the morning: outside the window, nothing but green fields, low hill bring horizon near. There is no beyond, not that way. In the kitchen he busies himself at the stove: Coffee from the stained stovetop Moka pot, milk warmed in a blue enamel saucepan. Toasted bread: raspberry jam from the grocery store.

He takes the second cup with him into the sitting room, opening the curtains over windows looking right onto the road. The cottage is too close to the road, but there's never any traffic to speak of. He glances at the small dining table by the window to the south: light is already falling on the books and notepad spread out across its surface. Dictionaries: source-book: references: he resumes work on the translation, regretting time stolen from his journal…

But what would he record? The crowded streets of Århus, with the flags and pennants gaily fluttering overhead, the improbable Baroque turrets, the carillons?   All the dark bronze men and mermaids, motionless, eternally poised within fountains, clutching swans or dragons, surrounded by flower-beds, or fastened to bronze prows at the ends of canals, gleaming in the sun, no bird-droppings spoiling their public beauty—

Or the zoo: apes grooming one another, eyeing their visitors critically: the polar bear diving sleek into his cold blue water: the elephants, wise and dignified even under the ridiculous straw heaps they toss onto their monumental heads?   The children's barnyard with its dutiful goats, calves, donkey, not to overlook the children themselves, sober now and aware of their responsibility to appear involved, interested, in process of being taught: and the adults, suspiciously out of place, looking on with apparent unconcern as if to mask the curiosity which in fact attends their gazes…

Objects in the room annoy him: a brass lamp, its stem too tall for the width of its base, the shape of its octagonal shade, vertical but curving out at the bottom like a sad woman's skirt, perched perilously close to the edge of the top shelf of the bookcase. The books themselves, all in Danish and most in sets of eight or ten or a dozen or more, uniformly bound and titled. Candlesticks: little pictures in easel mounts: statuettes: artificial flowers: bricabrac of the petit bourgeoisie. The bookshelf wall is plastered: the adjacent wall, whose windows illuminate his worktable, is brick, white brick with dark mortar, and the draperies, whose geometrical print — small exaggerated rectangles in those bright primary colors scattered across Scandinavia and the Low Countries in the wake of the CoBrA artists — the draperies complete the depressing, passively controlling work of the interior decorator, who had clearly delighted in a setting given to low ceilings, hard grainy surfaces, cold brass, irrelevant small presences.

In the corner a birch coat-rack, five feet tall, no more than two inches in diameter, with a crown of knobby truncated spokes angling out and up at the top: and not a hat to be seen.

She was up by now, had finished her coffee, had exchanged desultory conversation, had gone out. Blue sky: a few cottony cumulus clouds: it will be another fine day. She hangs a blue towel up to dry on the green plastic lines of the small revolving clothesline and looks out across the brown slats of the gate in the opening of the hedge surrounding the dooryard: beyond, sandy soil with a few weeds — dandelions and chamomile at best: otherwise simply weeds. She too has misgivings about the family across the road in the squat yellow stucco house under its sharply peaked roof, forming one side of a rectangle otherwise formed by the even lower cowbarn, the haybarn, and a couple of other outbuildings whose purpose was less apparent.

This is not the kind of dairy she'd lived on as a child. In California the cows live out of doors: her family's cows, scores of them, seemed like farmers themselves, spending the day in the fields, dutifully trooping back to the barn twice a day for that special feed, smelling both sweet and fermented, and giving their milk to the pulsing pumps and hoses. She had seen cows in the Alps who spent their summers like that, happily wandering pastures filled with flowers, ranunculus, wild rose, marigolds, crocus, the occasional gentian perhaps: there the milking machines went to the cows, there were no milk-barns: and the milk went to the *fromagerie* to cook in immense copper cauldrons. Tomme: Beaufort: Reblochon.

Here on the contrary things seemed dull and orderly, flat and low. It was beautiful, of course, and tranquil. But it was also humid: the grass sucked water perpetually up out of the ground, or funneled it back in, I suppose, on the occasions that it rained, though rain was what seemed never to happen, and one wondered what the source of the constant humidity could be, unless it was the cows themselves, endlessly drinking and pissing. Great bovine sacks of water, milk, and urine, dully chewing, dully gazing, constantly flicking their tails at the eternal flies.

3. I lift my eyes from the grass

THERE ARE ONLY two seasons, they call them "in" and "out." I can't be expected to know that, whatever knowing is, for me there is no memory, it all proceeds of its own accord. How could one be expected to have any kind of mental energy at all, to have learned about anything more complex than managing to eat, to lie down, to stand up again, to move about, to deal with the unpredictable subtle changes of light when a patch of white ambles past that thing too bright to look at, and too high. My neck hurts whenever I lift my eyes from the grass. Let others see the seagulls, I thank them without understanding for the soil and the grass. A poet far away will have written:

> *Mij, schaap, overkomt niets dan wat de herder wil,*
> *wat het gras wil, de lucht,*
> *wat de dam en de groene overkant.*
> *En ik tors mijn wol mee of het verlies van wol,*
> *kijk vol overgave uit mijn*
> *vochtige ogen. Ik ben gelukkig met wat ik heb.*
> *De tijd verstrijkt als gras, door mij,*
> *en elk verzet is hol. De bomen ruisen zinneloos.*

and I quite agree, only noting that sheep are low creatures, low to the ground, and so they cut the grass too close, leaving too little for the likes of me.

But what do I know. If I knew, I would know of cousins in distant lands, in the eternal "out" of California, on the improbable slopes of Savoie, standing in cool water up to their bellies under the cottonwoods in Oklahoma, hauling the plow in Philippine mud, where any turbulence is strictly conceptual, never experienced unless at the terrible last moment, the moment of which I am doomed — or thought — to be blissfully unaware, by virtue of my congenital idiocy.

Idiocy: etymologically, the condition of being wholly unconnected to any external reality.

De lucht, says the sheep, is it light or air, and is there any distinction. I cannot remember there being no light, no grass, the only sandy places are those laid bare by our steady footfalls, and there the chamomile is too close to the ground to taste. There is sweet grass all around: we graze: we stop: we lie down: we ruminate, they call it, we ruminate. What the farmer wants: we stand: we return: we give.

4. He is alone in the barn

HE LIFTS HIS eyes from the pages and rests them, looking out the window: in the grass well beyond, distant cows, brown and white, endlessly flick tails against perpetual flies. The noble and generous cow, he thinks, remembering a visit to a demonstration farm in Vermont, where a line of tourists waited turns at an attempt to milk a patient Guernsey in a fragrant stall.

He'd taken his turn, sat on the stool, laid his forehead against the flank, taken the teat between thumb and forefinger: and though it had been forty years his fingers and wrist recalled the stroke, the sweet and fragrant milk gladly sprayed its familiar tune against the stainless steel, a happy groundedness surged up from the straw-covered plank floor, through her hooves, her bones, her meat, her hair, his forehead, through his nerves and muscles and flesh back through the cotton of his trousers and the wooden stool and straw and planks in an endless cycle. Milking a cow resembles playing a piano, he thought, and returned his gaze to the papers. Skagen, in a few days, and the boat to Gothenburg, and there the train again, Örebro, Stockholm, Oslo, Bergen. The days and years, the rooms and the miles.

In the cowbarn the farmer feels his worn rubber boots, feels that they are worn and will soon need replacement, they can wait, they must wait, times are hard, the American visitors get on his nerves, they remind him of the unequal distribution of wealth.   He works steadily, seven days a week, the rhythm of his life as routine and predictable as the clock in his kitchen: what does he know of other lands, of airplanes, cities, languages.   He relishes resentment, it will do as substitute, rumination is his reward these days. What of his wife, his children. What of his dog, of the flies idly attending his wife as she bakes or boils, cleans, sets the house in order.

He is alone in the barn, where everything is in order, not that there's that much to be put in order. Stalls, stanchions, straw: the lamps hanging regularly from the ceiling-joists, the scent: straw, manure, mash, milk. A good smell that he hardly knows any more: his nose takes good for granted: it's simply another constant, like the flag hanging listlessly from the pole out the front door of the farmhouse, the door that rarely opens.   Even the Americans knew, intuitively no doubt, to come to the kitchen door.

Perhaps it's the same there.   On the other hand, why the brand-new leather book satchel: why the oddly blue cotton gabardine, his wife had told him, of his jacket: annoying, like the brash new Levis and the cowboy boots, like the dark dirty curls on his head.   His own hair was thinning and sandy, sandy in both senses.

The barn is in order: the hoppers are full of mash: the herd is healthy: the milking equipment clean and functioning. The weather is as it always is, the low sky warm against the humid flat pasture. Perhaps we'll take them out Sunday to the strand: visitors always like to look across the sea toward the west, where they've come from, and where they'll return, in a month it'll be as if they'd never arrived.

5. Hidden away there must be others

IS THERE AN OLD woman, she wonders, an old woman like those they used to have in attics or back bedrooms. Nowadays nursing homes. The ones in the corridors, in wheelchairs or leaning against walkers, those are generally silent, their eyes dull and blank. Hidden away there must be others, you hear them sometimes calling out, repeating indistinct names, help me, help me. Isolated. She polishes the sink to put thoughts away. Far in the cowbarn, Søster at school… no, school's out for the summer: Søster away with her girl friends, to the city. Another thought to put away. Along with thoughts about the American girl.

The American girl had been a bad idea. The girl herself isn't at fault, she's a nice girl, she tries to be helpful. But she's so… American. She's big: when she talks she makes mistakes, she simply doesn't fit in. When she tries to fit in she tries too hard: the effort swallows all of them, fills the room. Søster never liked her, not from the beginning, perhaps it's true as some had told her that your own children are resentful, they know they must share their home, their family, their friends, their *lives* even, and they even want to share, but they can't always be successful: and when they fail they are often angry or guilty, and that makes them resentful, and heaven knows adolescents are already resentful enough.

She sighs and dries the sink, remembering her own adolescence. It was hard not to be a resentful girl during the war, of course, but we all have the same history, the same excuse. And it was the years after the war that were hard. These girls will see, it doesn't matter how good they have it now, how good they think they have it, when they're older and they look back on it they'll think it should have been easier. She was confused, thinking about it. Are they resentful now, or will they be later: or is she putting her own thoughts in what she thinks their heads are. *What is that crazy man doing now.*

She's looked out the kitchen window: Far is striding across the yard carrying a heavy box. The sun is bright, no clouds in the sky, it's nearly noon, yet he wears his rubber boots and looks angry. Further off, in the pasture, what on earth could she be doing there, the American girl.

6. The American girl

THE AMERICAN GIRL is in a mood. The American girl is often in a mood. The word is "mood," she thinks, because the feeling is vague. She's not worried, she's not angry, she's not resentful, she's not even unhappy. She's not disappointed. Now that school is out, one day will slide easily into the next, as if there were no events, no relationships, no goals. It was simply a matter of the days sliding by until the one came that would put her on an airplane. Then things would change, but the American girl wasn't concerned about that. There was no way to know what the change would be. She would be home again, but she will have changed. For that matter, "home" will have changed.

Since there was no way to know *how* anything will have changed, there was no reason for the American girl to be concerned. She could look back on the last few months: it was easy to see what had changed, it was possible even to think about how it had changed, but there was no good reason to do that either. It had been hard much of the time. They had told her how hard many things about it might be, before she came. New language, new family, new school, no friends: everything starting over, a blank page to begin writing on. And to begin writing as she was told to write. She would be taking math, science, history, and language, right alongside everyone else, but they would have been in this school and this language since the beginning, and she was sixteen years old and had never been in this country, in this language, on this farm, ever before in her life.

The grass was not soft: it was short, chewn off, sharp and brittle. The ground wasn't soft either. It wasn't rock-hard, like the baked clay soil at home, but it wasn't soft and yielding. She looked down at her black leather shoes, nicely polished but a little worn, and her white socks, neatly turned down at the cuffs. She looked up at the thin clouds quietly sliding across the sun. She watched the cows grazing, flicking their tails, heads down, evenly scattered across the pasture, as if they knew how far apart to graze, which direction to face, when to lift their heads, gaze into the distance as if they were resting their eyes, slowly turn their heads to one side or the other, look sideways at one another, or at her, or at nothing, and then drop their heads again and resume grazing, tails flicking against the flies. The flies had stopped bothering her. If she brushed at her ear with a hand, or pursed her lips and blew upward at her nose, it was without thinking about it, perfectly unconscious. What a nice day. I wonder if Søster is having a nice day in town. I don't really care.

The American girl is disengaging: from the family, from the farm, from her parents even, who are in the cottage across the road, who may be expecting her to visit, who may be thinking about whether they should visit her in the farmhouse, who may not be thinking about her at all. They are part of the change. By leaving them for so many months she had changed them. That was how she knew that when she was home, home would be changed. Everything would be changed, maybe not in the same way her parents were changed, but as much as they were changed. That was a hard thing to think about. Her forehead wrinkled, she could feel that, it had wrinkled of its own accord, and she sighed and smoothed it out, not with her hands, just by relaxing it.   It was very hard to think about these things, especially on such a warm day.   It must be nice to be a cow, at least in the summer.

The American girl looked down at her notebook. So many notebooks.   She had tried to be careful to write things down, they had told her she'd be glad one day that she had, but by bedtime she was too tired, and before bedtime there were too many other things to do. At first she had written things down: names in her new family, names of places that seemed important for whatever reason, what time the bus would come to take her to school, names of teachers, assignments, difficult words or funny ones.   Later she noticed she was writing things in English, many of them names too, but names of things and people and places back home.   She'd noticed one day she couldn't remember her cousin's cat's name, and she knew it perfectly well.   She could *see* the cat, could almost hear its purr, but she'd forgotten its name. His name. It was Jack, of course, black Jack, don't slap back, they used to sing to him: and she wrote the name down in case she forgot it again, and thought about writing to her cousin that she'd forgotten Jack's name, but never got around to it.

The American girl was hungry, a little hungry. She knew it was lunchtime but she wasn't yet used to having lunch at home on a weekday and wasn't sure what she should do. Go in, as if she were expecting there to be a lunch?   Go in as if she were expecting to make lunch, her own lunch, or lunch for the others too?   Wait out here and see if someone called her to lunch?   She looked at the cows, grazing, completely unconcerned. It must be nice to know, always, exactly what to do.

She sighed, stood up, smoothed her clothes, put her notebook in her pocket, looked at the cows again, and walked slowly and carefully toward the house. Far in his rubber boots looked across the yard toward her, smiled, lifted a hand to beckon to her. Lunch time, then, it must be.

7. Another quiet strained evening

THE AMERICAN WOMAN took the blue towel from the clothesline, then stood there vacantly looking at the hedge. Yesterday, that bicycle ride to the seashore, and then to the farm. A long ride, maybe ten miles, against a wind — is that an offshore wind? — to meet a woman who was apparently important somehow: and then to the farm she lived on. Everyone here seems to be a farmer. The village was small and picturesque, big houses and small ones scattered on hillsides with no apparent logic, one of those big stone churches with a tall narrow steepgabled roof, a big wooden windmill on the ridge, flagpoles, ropes slapping them in the wind. Nothing by way of gardens: grass, armeria, The dunes are probably too poor a soil for anything more.

Some of the buildings rather colorful, yellow-beige or dark red: most spanking clean white. But my god what do these people do? No shops or offices to be seen: how do they support themselves? Fishing, probably, or providing for fishermen. And farming, of course. The beach is nice, of course: it was pleasant to stand there and look out toward England, invisible, and think about Ireland beyond, and then Newfoundland I suppose. The ugly concrete bunker, like a stranded pigsnouted whale, left there because too difficult to destroy it? Or it may be useful one day again?

The site of the old church, the new church, the school, then to the farm. Brings back memories. Lots of pigs, a couple each of goats, cows, horses, sheep, rabbits. Coffee, cake, buttered rolls, and cookies, a look at his Russian car — why is that special, I wonder. Does he show it to us to make fun of our politics. And then his horse, a mare being bred, the stallion brought to him by a neighbor with a horse-trailer behind his car, and small boys looking on mischievously from a nearby copse of birches.

What a long day. The ride home, this time *with* the wind. Still, good thing I'd brought a scarf to tie over my ears. Pork chops, rice, the rest of yesterday's prune pudding, ice cream with pineapple slices. And another quiet strained evening: I know he wants to get back to his translations, but we have to visit, to be polite, even though they must surely be as tired as we, and as eager for bed.

She turned quickly, abruptly, and stepped back into the house, crumpling a corner of the towel in her left hand, turning the doorknob with her right. He was at his worktable, a mug of coffee at his hand. He looked up, asked a question with his eyebrows, got no answer, looked back down to his books. She stepped into the kitchen and hung the towel on its hook, thinking about lunch. Yesterday we'd had that omelet — a bit like Finnish pancake, butter and flour and eggs, with tomato and cucumber slices scattered on top, not a good match she thought. And strawberries thickened with cornstarch, with milk poured on top. She thought of the fruit soup they'd so often had when they were young and poor, plums from the ornamental red-leafed trees that grew between sidewalk and curbstone, stewed with a little sugar and thickened with rice or tapioca or cornstarch, maybe a few raisins, a stick of cinnamon. She couldn't remember whether they'd added milk, or half-and-half, or not. She wished there were a jar of peanut butter in the cabinet. Tuna, then, a can of tuna, there was mayonnaise in a jar, there were pickles, god knows there were pickles.

8. The myth of memory and the moment

TRANSLATING IS HARD work, you could say, or you could say that it's not really all that hard. And it gets easier as it goes along, at least for a while: at some point you hit a snag, everything bogs down for a while, then it gets easier again, you're on a downhill glide. It's like riding a bicycle through the countryside, wind at your back. You crank her a bit to get up to the top of a rise, then you coast for a while if you like. If you keep cranking, at least it's easier. Effortless, almost.

Translating's like that. After all it's mostly a matter of reading something you're already interested in, otherwise why bother, in a language you already know something about. If you're lucky you'll hit a sequence of three or four sentences that practically translate themselves, clear expository writing. Now and then there's an unfamiliar word, and you look it up. It doesn't hurt to have an etymological dictionary as well as the two others, the French-English English-French dictionary and the only French dictionary.

Of course there are other traps. Slang, for example, or casual language, you have to be alert for that: but it doesn't come up often in this kind of work. Idioms are another matter. It's easy to fall into the trap of translating something literally. Old joke, current when the first computer translation was attempted: man types "out of sight, out of mind" into machine to turn it into Russian: machine translates it into Russian, then back into English to check it: "invisible and insane."

He sighs, looks at his watch, returns his gaze to the book: *The Myth of Memory and the Moment.* The book's under his left hand, open to an early page, somewhere in the thirties. Under his right hand a pad of unlined rather nice paper he'd bought on a previous trip — somewhere in Savoie, no, the Chartreuse, two years ago, the summer he'd had a wisdom tooth pulled in a small town, St. Laurent du Pont, a sad town, or rather a town with a sad history: in the 1940s or '50s there'd been a tragic fire in a night club, scores of deaths.

He's thinking now about French newspapers, which has nothing to do with the day's assignment. Those thin newspapers in the provinces, with their reports on sports, the winning lottery numbers, the weather predictions. Usually a scare story with a happy ending: a child falls off a third-floor balcony but is caught, or lands in shrubbery, unharmed. A dog warns a sleeping couple their house is on fire. A car is swept away by rising waters in a rainstorm: the driver escapes injury. No doubt the newspapers are the same here, but he hasn't seen any: no point in it: he doesn't know Danish. He doesn't even know French, he reflects, turning back to Suquet.

The American girl is his daughter. My daughter is an American girl, he thinks, living in a Danish family, on a farm, a dairy farm, in Jutland. "Jutland," he thinks, not "Denmark," and is distracted by this new distinction. It's not like him to be hellbent for specificity. "Denmark" would do just as well. It's just that the country has seemed so fragmented, so broken up by its waters: the waters part the country as the point at Skagen will soon be seen to part the seas. It's not a country of long vistas, apparently: low hills block the horizon: the country roads proceed by gentle curves and slopes, not straight lines: the towns and cities are broken up by church-towers and apartment buildings, never more than a dozen storeys or so, scattered among the one- and two-storey buildings, brick or stucco, the roofs steep. Step gables. Lead-roofed cupolas. Young trees planted in rows, each with a careful tripod of clean unpainted wood, birch no doubt, angling up from the pavement to a wooden girdle with rubber, maybe leather straps supporting the saplings against a sudden wind-blast, though the weather has been calm and dry and warm, cottony white clouds mostly for decoration in the improbably blue sky.

His daughter was American, but she had clearly changed. Grown, matured, dealt with difficulties. And she speaks Danish: when she turns to her Danish mother and converses easily with her it's as if she has gone away, has suddenly been exchanged — yes, that's the word — for a stranger, a girl who looks familiar in every way except for whatever detail it is you most want to fix on: her smile: her eye: certain gestures. The set of her head when she says Yes or No, *Ja* or *Nej* is it? Most of all, when a comment is apparently made referring to him, and they turn and glance at him, smiling in a friendly way, and then resume their conversation, and the friendly smile was the kind strangers make to one another, not intimate friends or family relatives.

That had been clear on the first visit, the day they'd arrived in the taxi, there being no train service to this little village, fortunately only a few miles from the station. They'd tumbled out of the taxi at the farmhouse, got their bags out of the trunk — two suitcases, her big straw bag, his paper shopping-bag. (Got to get a decent briefcase or something next time in town.) A rush of greeting, broken English, awkward silences, much clumsiness, barking dog. Lucky they'd found a place for us: no awkward trooping up a narrow staircase to a tiny bedroom, probably belonging to one of the children, temporarily bunking elsewhere and resenting it. The girls arrived later, when school was out, and there was the quick joyful reunion after nearly a year since last they'd seen her, quickly marred, he thinks, by the awareness that she had changed, grown, grown away, was no longer entirely an American girl. How did she manage that? How was she able to be neither American nor Danish, both at home and homeless?

He was aware of another distance, between him and his wife: each of them had quite a different response to this, or, rather, quite a different way of processing what was very likely the same response, or a very similar one: after all they were father and mother to the same American girl, were alike in seeing that she had grown away from them, but he was pleased that she'd distanced herself from America, and he wasn't sure that his wife was pleased with that, or aware of it. She certainly knew that he felt this way, but she probably felt that he was mistaken: the girl hadn't distanced herself from her country, her home town, her real family: not really: she'd simply adapted to the new country and the farm and her exchange family. That was an achievement. She doubted that *she* could have done that when she was sixteen. But it was a temporary accommodation: in fact the girl wasn't changed at all: she was the same daughter she'd always been, and would return in a few months, and resume the girlhood she'd been so comfortable with all these years.

9. She turns to look behind

THE GRASS GROWS indistinct, harder to see, harder to see each blade as a separate leaf. But easier to smell. The smell had changed. The smell of the earth was a little more pungent, the smell of the grass a little less sharp. And the other smell, that comes only now and then when the grass is easier to see, that smell was sharper now. Well, not sharper, it was a very soft smell, but there was something sharp under it, like the big cube thing that is sharp and grainy when you lick it. It was time to go in.

She got slowly and ponderously to her feet, rear first, then fore, and lifted her head a little, rolling her eye, turning her head to the left. There were no flies for the moment. The others were getting up too. She coughed, lifted her tail, peed, a huge stream, her back arched, looking sideways at the others: then she slowly turned and began walking toward the barn. The others followed. The thing at her neck made its noise: it always did: she hardly noticed it any more.

The way went gently uphill at first, then gently down: you could hardly notice the change, but she was heavy. It doesn't really grow dark, but the air is heavier, the sounds muffled, the smells changed and softer. The earth feels softer too, as if it would give a little under foot, but it's hard to be sure that's really true, perhaps it's only the hour.

It takes several minutes. She doesn't really see the barn: she doesn't lift her head: she knows it's there, where it always has been, always will be.   When she reaches the gravel though she stops, as if to consider.   The dog stands at the doorway, anxious, excited, foolish, stepping this way, then that, then returning to the doorway, its tail constantly in motion though there are no flies. The man must be inside. She turns to look behind: the others have come up and stopped too, not wanting or not able to pass her, keeping their assigned places in line. She makes a little noise with her throat, tosses her head a little from side to side, and goes on into the barn.

Completely different smell: hay, feed, milk, electricity, metal. A little bit of dog, a little bit of man. She walks on quietly, with certainty and reserve, and steps onto the little platform and puts her head in the metal thing. The others must be doing the same thing: she can't see them, but she hears and smells. The feed is sweet and sticky and her big wet rough tongue scrapes it into her mouth while something happens underneath, warm, wet: then the milk begins to flow.   Her tail flicks at occasional flies.   The electricity hums, something pulses, the feed is sweet, it's all the way it always is.

The dog looks up at Far and smiles happily. Everything in place. He yawns and goes out into the twilight: his dish will be ready soon. A cat watches him leave, then stretches and begins his rounds among the cows.

10. A man who knew things

DINNER WENT WELL: good thing. Far was pleased with the meat. The Americans don't eat very much and they are slow, moving their forks and knives around all the time, putting them down and taking them up again. And they don't seem to be able to talk while they eat, it's either one thing or the other. How did they become so important and so rich, when they always seem so slow and so stupid. She shouldn't think that of course, they can't be stupid, not as stupid as they seem anyway, they are probably confused, as their girl was when she first came. The first month or two she had thought the American girl was incredibly stupid, you can hardly imagine why they would choose her to send away, the others must be terrible if they are even more stupid. But then she realized, or maybe her Far had reminded her, the poor girl doesn't understand a word she hears, she has to begin from the very beginning, like a newborn, but she must weigh nearly sixty kilo and it's hard to remember her mind is so small and new when her body is so big and, well, certainly not new.

The one troubling thing in this setup is probably Far, how perfect he should be named Far. "Troubling" may be too strong a word. But even Translator, who is normally quite sanguine, composed, almost phlegmatic, found something not quite right about Far. Clearly this was a man who knew things, who had stories at his command: but he held them back: he never told his stories. Far was quiet and disengaged to the point of rudeness. Sure: he speaks no

English, and doesn't understand really how to listen to interpreters.   He looks at you when you speak, uncomprehending, and continues to look at you when the American girl translates, as if what she's doing is irrelevant, a nuisance even, as meaningful to the evening's attempt at conversation as the cat is to the milking.   You'd forgive anyone thinking he was simply stupid: but if you watch him at other times, when there is no attempt at conversation, during the quiet moments at table or afterward (and there are many quiet moments), you might see him looking into a distance, listening to a story you can't hear, you won't hear. And if you could see him going about his business, tending to the milking parlor, the silo, the grain-bin, walking the pastures with his dog at his heel, eyeing the cows — why then you'd see this is a very competent man, not stupid at all.

Unless "stupid" is the word you use for a man who's simply inarticulate, whose life and business have no particular relationship to conversation, to *any* verbal communication. He follows some other principle of order.   Spending his long working hours with the herd, the dog, the grass, the barn, he has no need for words: he's fallen out of the habit of using them.   His stories have come to him through his eyes, except for those he'd heard in his childhood.   You can't send them back out again through your eyes: the stories stay with him.

There's the matter of his age, for one thing.   If he was twelve, say, at the end of the war, then you might imagine he had no real awareness of what the war had meant, of what his family, his neighbors, his teachers had done, had had to do, during those years.   But he might be older than he looks: he might have been fifteen or even sixteen by the time the war had ended and Germans had given way to the others and then it was Denmark again.   In that case he would have seen and heard things that he'd had to make some kind of sense of. If you experience such things without making sense of them they continue to disturb you. He was not a man given to disturbance.

There didn't seem to be that many people around here. Far didn't seem to have or to need friends, associates, even family beyond his own, and now the American girl of course. No doubt there were business dealings: accounts, purchases of feed and equipment, contracts with cheese and butter producers who bought his milk. Fuel for the tractor and the car: an account at the grocery store (that would have been minor): maybe visits concerned with health, doctors, the dentist. Who cut his hair? His wife, probably.

What was troubling was the notion that Far was a man who knew things, whose stories mattered, conveyed historical information. The region was compromised, and now it seems innocent and tranquil. Why is it so sparsely populated? What happened to previous generations? The old men — the one who paints, the net-mender who smokes his pipe: the preacher even, at the church in the village at the dunes: what do they know? Where were they: who did they associate with?

And what about the women? How many of them slept with the enemy in the terrible (or at least uncomfortable) months of no milk, no eggs, no flour or butter, nothing but what you'd hidden in the cellar, or what you could beg from neighbors more fortunate than yourself? How much had they had to keep secret from their children, their men, one another?

11. The only reason he asks

THEY ALWAYS ASK the same two questions: does it snow here. Well, yes, of course it snows here: it's normal to have snow in winter, don't you think?   There's hardly a corner of the continent that doesn't see snow at least once in a winter. The weather is as it always is. And then, a little later, as if to take you by surprise except that you've heard it a hundred times before: what was it like here during the war. Of course you can't blame them, I suppose, the war didn't touch their country. God knows they sent plenty of their boys to die in it: they sent their ships and airplanes and tanks and guns, and later their cigarettes and chocolate, and they took some of our women and left others with babies. But the war didn't touch their country, that's the thing, they had no idea of the hardest part of the war, the occupation, the collaboration, the need to continue daily life with the gun at your back, the disapproval, the suspicion, the betrayals, hungry most of the time, and cold. Indeed it snows here.

Even after the war, when every now and then someone went missing, perhaps to be found a week or a month or even a year later, in a ditch or a pond, and you remember how people had looked at him during the war, how they'd fallen silent if he walked past, say returning from the bakery with two loaves of bread, or another was seen smoking a factory cigarette, or a girl had a warm wool coat she couldn't explain. Oh I found it in a truck whose tires had gone flat, she might say, or Oh it was my aunt's, you've seen it before, don't you remember it?

We didn't have such things of course. No one in our family had any luck that way, not the good luck to find anything useful or the bad luck to know anyone well enough to turn some little profit out of the situation. We ate some of the cows, two of them I think, and turned others over as they were requisitioned, and it was just as well, there wasn't enough feed to maintain the herd, the poor cows had to look out for themselves just like the rest of us. Only the cats seemed to do well. Even the dogs grew thin and anxious. The old people, the grandparents, they remembered the last one, they mostly said it was even worse then, though the fighting hardly touched us the hard times were just as bad. But there are times it's best to live on the edge of things, far from the real fighting, from the factories and the railyards and the harbors.

If they ask what the war was like when they visit Paris or Berlin, or Rotterdam, for heaven's sake, then they'll get an ear full. Uncle had a friend in Rotterdam: no one ever heard from him again. Gone there in '34 to work in the harbor, nothing but money to be made there he said, and even sent some back to Uncle, probably paying off a loan, Uncle was a soft touch. But after the bombing no one heard from him. How many have disappeared without leaving a trace. You don't find *them* in ditches or ponds: they're gone without leaving a trace. Far knew him, he was only a little boy then but he remembers him, but he doesn't talk about it. No reason to tell the American. He has his own story of how things were though he's not even old enough to know anything about it. The only reason he asks is, he thinks he already knows.

12. The point of view of the bunker

HE PROBABLY SHOULD have gone to the beach with them, but he was eager to continue working, the tempo was good, not a good idea to stop when things are running smoothly. Anyway dunes. And picnics. Still, too bad to miss terrain you haven't seen, how likely is it we'll be back here. But there's Skagen, the promise of Skagen, a Special Place. The one thing is, the bunker. Like a beached whale, she said, a whale with the snout of a pig. Curious image.

What would it be like — suppose, just for the exercise, you were to try to see things from the point of view of the bunker. Of course who knows what actually may have happened. For that matter, when were they built? And who built them? The Germans, no doubt. When did they occupy Denmark? Must have been early in the game: 1940? And did they expect an invasion, that they built bunkers like that? Stranded, she said, on the beach: but they must have been under the bluffs, covered with the dunes, and perhaps the sand has blown off them over the years. The bunker itself, grey beached whale, would know nothing about who had made it, or when. Dull concrete, poured in wood-boarded forms, reinforced with mesh no doubt, or rebar, if they had rebar then. Should learn something about the history of concrete. God knows he'd mixed enough of it: mixer-loads, four shovels of mix, one of cement, when he was in high school working for Uncle Lester. Fenceposts in Los Angeles when he was in college there: they rolled chicken wire into tight cylinders and filled them with concrete, slathering it on. Later, when they were dry enough, they set them up in shallow post-holes, and wired sheets of chicken wire to them, say four inches apart, four feet high, and filled the space with more concrete. Jerry-built concrete wall: I bet it's long since crumbled into dust.

Bunker: empty alone and silent for decades now. Once there were men, shouting and sweating, getting along together it seemed but hating the one in charge, nailing planks to posts, the hammering going on all day. Then the mixing, sand and gravel and pungent dusty grey cement, and wheelbarrows and more sweat and shouting. Finally finished and left to dry out. Always the noise of the sea and the gulls, whether the men were there or not. Warm, even while still wet: a different kind of warm after dried out. Then cool, always cool, the air never again touching the sides. The men come back and make it light inside, day and night it's still light inside when the men are there, but when they leave it's dark inside, night or day. And the sea and the gulls are quieter, perhaps they've left entirely. The men go, the men come back, like the tides and the gulls: but after many such intervals they're gone and they don't come back. Always dark. The ladder is gone, the machinery is gone. At very long intervals a sound of some kind, scratching usually, sometimes a hollow booming. Then one day it is light again, the little hole at the top sees the sky again, a small man is there, he turns his face away and shouts, another joins him, then another. Stones dropping, and the echo of the noise when they strike the floor, and the shouting. Then silence, but not darkness: and then, later, darkness, with little points of light: and then for a while alternations of light and darkness, the boys as they call them returning time to time. And great shiftings and rollings, and the sides warm again as they were at first, and the sea and the gulls again, louder at first until their noise is familiar again, and quieter voices, not shouting but murmuring, and occasional wet splashes against the sides and laughing. Odd to know these things, to hear them, to feel them, but never to see except the light and the darkness alternating, and the little points of light above.

And so the years go by, like the gulls and the waves.

He sighs and pushes away the papers.   A ridiculous exercise: but any more ridiculous than any other?   Futility is what you make of it. Better: futility is where you find it. That's it. Futility is where you find it. Sigh, and think of Skagen.

13. The machinery is clean

SHE THOUGHT OFTEN of her father, dead these dozen years. A fine, quiet, intelligent man, essentially optimistic though always close to poverty, scratching at a living however he could — fishing, clerking at the chandlery, repairing things. She thought of his hands, huge hands for so small a man, and stained, and stiff and knotted in his last thirty years, when he'd gone from the middle-aged man she first knew to the frail old man he became at the last. His glasses cloudier with scratches and neglect.

She thought much less often of her mother, who had gone first, when she was only a girl. Perhaps that's *why* she thought of her less: she hadn't had time to make that much impression on her: had left very little influence, though Far always said she looked like her, not at all like her father since she was tall and fair and he was short and darker, or was it the tobacco that had made his face so dark. At the end he still had his pipe, always his pipe with him, though for years he'd not lit it, and toward the end not even bothered with tobacco, just the pipe. When she was a girl there had been four of them, carved briar pipes with yellowed stems, standing ready in the wooden rack he'd made for them, with a box of matches and a curious knife, on the little end-table by his chair, with a door on its lower shelf: the tobacco can was always on the shelf, out of the light but its blue label faded nonetheless, you could hardly make out the words though the picture was still clear, a fisherman in his longbilled hat standing in a dory.

She thought he'd probably always wished she'd been a boy.
She stood next to him at his workbench, not much of a
workbench really, smelling the shavings, sweeping them up
from the board floor and throwing them into the stove,
wishing she could learn to carve, to use the fretsaw, to make
things: wishing he could somehow teach her: but there was
no possibility of that: he had no idea how to engage her, to
lay out any kind of instruction in terms clear and orderly
enough to transmit to her. Their minds were parallel but
somehow disconnected. He knew things she would never
know, would never imagine; would never know, even, that
she didn't know them. There are things, he told her more
than once, that you can't really know: you can only know
that you don't know them. Perhaps someone else knows
them. In some cases *I* might even know them, but you
don't, and you won't, and you won't even know that you
don't. And it's funny, we call them "things," though they
might not be things at all, they might be only ideas, or
memories, or lies, or stories, or suspicions, or mistakes —
things that aren't things at all, that have no substance and
are only pictures you can't see, or voices you can't hear, that
exist only inside your head. Not *your* head, of course, since
you don't know them: but perhaps *my* head, or your
mother's (though I don't think that's likely), or the
predicant's.

He would be carving something when he talked like that, or
gluing something together, or taking something apart, a
clock or a lamp or something of that sort, or putting it back
together again. He always cleaned it first. Methodically,
using a stiff brush if necessary, or a bit of cotton from a
worn shirt. He always cleaned things dry. The cloth would
not be damp: there was no place for water on his
workbench. Sometimes he might use a drop or two of light
oil: if so, then he would finish with a polishing cloth. She
liked both the looks and especially the smell of the clean

brass, the white birch or pine, the scraped and lightly oiled workbench. When the shavings went into the stove there was the smell of ash, though months would go by without a fire. Odd: the ash smells more like the brass than the shavings. Sometimes the feed in the bins smells like that: or, really, it's the bins that smell like that, the smell is stronger when they're empty of feed, not that that happens very often.

It would be nice if Far had a workbench like that, if he carved wood, clean birch or pine, to make pegs for hanging the coats, or holders for the brooms in the closet. Of course we're not lacking for hooks. The barn, the porch, the kitchen, they're all supplied with plenty of hooks, nice strong metal ones, but it's not the same. You don't complain, of course. Far works hard, and times have changed. Well, he doesn't work as hard as they did in the old days, but he works long hours, all day. You don't unload burlap sacks of feed from the truck these days, it comes in bigger trucks that blow it up into the feed bin automatically. You don't throw bales any more: electricity does the heavy lifting. But he works long hours, from first milking through the late milking, watching, worrying, weighing. There are plenty of ways to be a good man, and if today's ways are different from the old ways, they're no less honest.

One thing hard to remember: the workbench itself: had he made it too? Or was it something he'd got from his own father? Maybe it had been handed down over a couple of generations. He never talked about his own father, or his grandparents. Funny about that, why hadn't she asked him? Had she been aware somehow, without knowing it, that it was a subject he didn't want to discuss? He was young when his father died, the dates are in the family Bible, but the handwriting's hard to make out, the ink's faded. Yes: seem to remember hearing that the workbench

had been his father's, maybe even his grandfather's.   It
wasn't factory-made, that's certain. Not a screw or a bolt in
it, except maybe where the new vise had been attached to
the front.   It was all pegged together, pegged and glued,
innocent of metal, or nearly. The metal was reserved for
the tools: above all, the sharp shining chisels standing in
their wood-strip pockets along the back of the workbench,
blades down, knobby handles at the top, their flattened
sides against the back plank. Flattened, probably, so they
wouldn't roll when they were laid down on the workbench.
In the rack they seemed alert, almost alive, waiting to bite
the birch or the pine. If you could smell the edge, honed to
finger-slice sharp, it would smell like a young lemon, the
kind you buy early in the year at the market. The chisel
spends its life waiting.   Ready, competent, but waiting,
hardly ever working. When it *does* work it works quickly and
fairly quietly, and the result is those curly shavings that she
sweeps up for the stove.   But it works rarely.   The jack
plane, now it works more often, and it's really a chisel too, a
blade in a block of wood. It seems less intelligent, duller —
not in terms of the sharpness of its blade, there's no doubt
about how sharp it is: but it's thick and cloddy, not graceful
and attentive like the chisels: and of course it can't stand in
a wood-strip pocket, it can only sit dully on the workbench,
invariably in the way when something's to be done there.

You can't blame Far for not working like that at a bench.
His gift is for organizing, timing, supervising. The bin is
never empty: just before it would be empty the truck arrives
to blow feed into it, full to the top. The machinery is clean
and runs perfectly: nothing ever needs to be repaired.
Before any part of it fails, a replacement part has been
ordered, has been delivered, has been put away on a shelf
ready to be put into place. The milk runs through its
tubing into the cooler, into the cans, ready to be picked up
by the truck that never fails to arrive, even if there's snow.

In the summer the cows come and go as they're meant to, without thinking, without being ordered, though the dog does his best to seem important. In the winter they stand or lie patiently in their places, healthy and uncomplaining, there only to be useful to us.

And when they're no longer useful, when they no longer give milk?

14. The special geographical point

NAPE OF THE NECK. Crook of the elbow: palm of the hand: sole of the foot: pit of the belly: bridge of the nose: hair of the head: tilt of the chin does not count: nape of the neck.

Tilt of the chin, set of the mouth, rise of the eyebrow, flare of the nostrils, narrowing of the eyes, shrug of the shoulders, clench of the fist.

Out the window the hedge. The window itself, the glass of the window is not perfectly transparent, it interposes its own substance on the view. Something always comes between the eye and the object. The cast of the eye: the haze of the window. He knew how vision works: light bounces off the object, is focused by the cornea, strikes rods and cones on the retina where the configuration of the focussed light is turned into nervous electricity and sent to a specialized area of the brain, where the nervous electricity is resolved into some kind of nervous activity in response. Oh yes: that's a familiar object: or Oh look, never seen that before. The glass of the window simply one more filter in the process. You learn to look past the filters. A question of priorities: the object, or the filters, or the configuration, or the activity, or the response. The eye of the beholder. Cut of the jib.

The evenings are long at this latitude, or is it jet lag. He prefers to ignore jet lag, to pretend it does not affect him. The excitement of arrival overcomes the discomfort of flight, but the next day, the next few days, that's when

adjustment necessarily takes place.   It's not as foreign as
he'd anticipated.   There is a constant juggling: English and
Danish: the scale of the streets and the buildings (less
apparent here in the country): unfamiliar people and
customs contrasted with the continuity of his work, brought
with him, always proceeding faster in Europe, where it's
free from interruptions from the office, the students, friends
and family.   The evenings are long and it grows dark late.
Next week it will be even more pronounced, traveling from
Oslo to Bergen on a night of full moon: planned for that
reason.   The special geographical point, the Claw of
Skagen: then the special midsummer full moon as far north
as possible.   Anything afterward, everything afterward, can
take care of itself.   Let events unfold at their own pace, like
the flight of light from object to the mind.   Meaning is
where you find it.

A small glass of akvavit stood at the right of the notebook.
It stood out clearly from the background, but so did the
pen, the bottle of ink, the small stapler from the stationer in
Copenhagen.   All those hard and shiny objects, unlike the
others: the pad of white paper, gummed at the top edge, a
few pages folded underneath, the exposed page half filled
with careful calligraphy.   The spiralbound notebook,
opened, the cover folded back exposing a blank graphpaper
page.   The book, closed now, a dark blue ribbon marking a
page.   The black leather pocket agenda.   The light
changed: half a moon had moved into the rectangle of
glass, glass known to be slightly hazy but clear enough for a
sudden revelation: the moon high in its frame: lower,
reflected in the glass against the darkened yard outside, the
white shade of the table lamp, white with a slight yellow
cast from the lamp bulb. Time to close the notebook, close
the pad, put all aside for the night, suspend all thought until
the morning. Shank of the night.

15. Milk. Plastbelagt. Signs

IN COPENHAGEN A WOMAN buys a half-liter of milk in one of those little supermarkets. When she opens it, back in her apartment, the milk doesn't look right. It doesn't smell right either. In fact it is spoiled. This is odd, as the milk has been ultrapasteurized, or perhaps irradiated, who knows what they do to the milk these days, it doesn't even have to be kept refrigerated any more, nothing can happen to it. They say. She'd taken it off the shelf where it stood alongside a number of identical containers, cardboard boxes treated with something, not paraffin as used to be the case, plastic of some sort no doubt, yes, she recalls the odd word she's heard, *plastbelagt*. "Plasticized" we call it, he said.

She went back to the store to complain, but lost her nerve. Anyway, she'd forgotten to bring the box of milk. She looked at the shelf: the same boxes, standing in the same configuration. She noticed though that the sign was wrong. ÆLK, it said, instead of *mælk*, as if in English a sign over a milk case had been lettered ILK, the "m" missing. Issing.

It fell off probably: there was a space where it should have been, the other letters were apparently glued on to the plastic sign in whatever fashion. She stood looking at the plastic sign, stepping aside to let another lady reach for a half-liter of ilk. Should she say anything to her, she wondered, considering the question, she looked nice enough in her dark wool sweater and pleated skirt, rather a plain face but pleasant enough, but she didn't know her, had never seen her before: it could be awkward to open a conversation, especially when the subject would necessarily be unpleasant: she probably wouldn't want to hear, wouldn't believe her, and perhaps she was wrong anyway, how could it have been spoiled, nothing can happen to it. She sighed and walked slowly along the aisle, past the cold case, the packaged cheeses, the cans of things, around the end of the shelves and back toward the front of the store again, ignoring the inadequate selection of fruits and vegetables, the paper goods, the bottles of wine and akvavit, the atches and candles, scrubbers and gloves, can openers and paring knives, none very good. Everything was in order, all the signs correct. She thought of going back to look at the dairy shelves again but didn't want to backtrack, it wasn't done, one doesn't walk the wrong direction in such shops.

On the other hand one also doesn't leave the shop without a purchase, and there was nothing she really needed, certainly nothing she wanted. Still. A candle is always a good thing to have: she took the first one she saw, a short white stubby thing, and found a few coins in her bag, and paid, and left quickly, too quickly. She had never felt so nervous. Still she did not take the first bus to arrive at the stop but let it go by even though it was not at all full. She stood at the bus stop as the evening dragged on and waited for the next bus. When it arrived she got on, easily finding a seat near the exit, holding the candle which she'd put in her pocket exactly as if instead of paying for it she had stolen it. Her face reddened at the thought.

Translator's notes

I know little about the French author Jean Coqt, whose typescript of *Skagen: un roman de l'Europe* I found in a used-book shop in Grenoble. The proprietor of the shop thought he was a Savoyard, perhaps from near Bilignin : that he was born in the 1920s or 1930s — *"après de la guerre, sûrement"* — and that he was no longer living. A shy man, he had left the manuscript with the bookseller for advice, and never returned. Internet searches have turned up nothing.

I have tried to translate the original faithfully, but the original French is idiosyncratic, and some curious lapses in style have resulted.

Page 8, *A poet far away will have written:* the poet is the Dutch Mark Boog, whose poem, found engraved on a stone in a Limburg pasture near Epen, I translate, not idiomatically:

ME, SHEEP

Me, sheep, nothing comes up but what the shepherd wants
what the grass wants, the air,
what the dam and the green beyond.

And I shoulder my wool or my loss of wool,
and I look out diligently from my
moist eyes. I'm happy with what I have.

Time passes like grass, through me,
and any opposition is hollow. The trees rustle sinless.

Page 22, Suquet: the French poet, writer, and photographer Jean Suquet (1928-2007).

Page 32, Rotterdam: the heart of the Dutch seaport was almost completely destroyed on May 10, 1940, by German bombers.

set in Baskerville and Deco Type Naskh

ear : press : 2014

www.ingramcontent.com/pod-product-compliance
Lightning Source LLC
Chambersburg PA
CBHW050907120626
46554CB00003B/1064